Katie's Picture Show

James Mayhew

ORCHARD

To Rosemary, with love and thanks

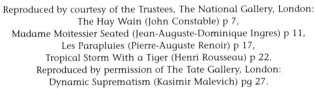

Reproduced by courtesy of the Trustees, The National Gallery, London:
The Hay Wain (John Constable) p 7,
Madame Moitessier Seated (Jean-Auguste-Dominique Ingres) p 11,
Les Parapluies (Pierre-Auguste Renoir) p 17,
Tropical Storm With a Tiger (Henri Rousseau) p 22.
Reproduced by permission of The Tate Gallery, London:
Dynamic Suprematism (Kasimir Malevich) pg 27.

ORCHARD BOOKS
338 Euston Road, London NW1 3BH
Orchard Books Australia
Level 17/207 Kent Street, Sydney, NSW 2000
First published in 1989 by Orchard Books
First published in paperback in 1991
This edition published in 2004
ISBN 978 1 84362 397 7
Text and illustrations © James Mayhew 1989
Cover illustrations © James Mayhew 2004
The right of James Mayhew to be identified as the author and illustrator of
this work has been asserted by him in accordance with the
Copyright, Designs and Patents Act, 1988.
A CIP catalogue record for this book is available
from the British Library.
9 10 8
Printed in China
Orchard Books is a division of Hachette Children's Books,
an Hachette UK company.
www.hachette.co.uk

Katie and her Grandma were in London for the whole day. When it started to rain Grandma said, "Let's go into the art gallery and look at some pictures."

Katie took Grandma in through a big revolving door (the one marked 'No Entry', of course), spinning her round and round at least seven times.

NO ENTRY

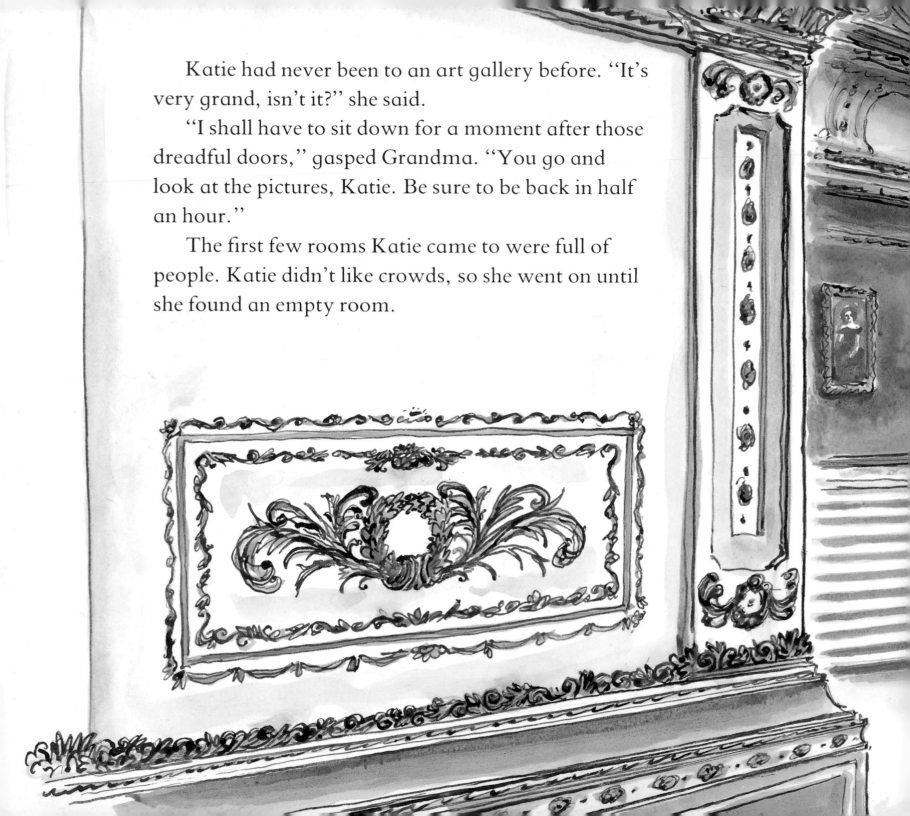

Katie had never been to an art gallery before. "It's very grand, isn't it?" she said.

"I shall have to sit down for a moment after those dreadful doors," gasped Grandma. "You go and look at the pictures, Katie. Be sure to be back in half an hour."

The first few rooms Katie came to were full of people. Katie didn't like crowds, so she went on until she found an empty room.

There were lots of pictures in the room. Katie didn't know which one to look at first. She stopped in front of a painting of a horse-drawn cart.

The Hay Wain by John Constable, she read.
PLEASE DO NOT TOUCH.

"Why not?" said Katie, poking a rather dirty finger at the picture. To her surprise, it went right past the frame and into the painting.

"This isn't a picture at all," cried Katie, astonished. "It's real!" Then, looking carefully around her, she climbed *right into the painting*!

"This is fun!" said Katie. She marched off through the mud towards a cottage. A delicious smell of cooking came from an open window.

Katie found a freshly-baked apple pie cooling on the window sill. She helped herself to a rather large slice. It was such a good apple pie that she ate the rest as well.

"Hey, that was my supper," shouted one of the men on the cart. His dog started to bark at Katie and she thought it would be best to leave. She ran back to the picture frame and climbed down into the gallery.

Katie peered round the doorway of the next room. There was a guard sitting next to the door, but he was asleep.

Katie went up to the painting she liked best.
Jean-Auguste-Dominique Ingres, she read. PLEASE DO
NOT TOUCH. But, of course, she did.

"Hullo, I'm Katie," said Katie to a lady sitting beside a mirror.

"*Enchantée!*" replied the lady. "I am Madame Moitessier."

"What a lovely dress," said Katie politely. "Are you French?"

"*Mais oui!*" replied Madame Moitessier. "And very lonely. We sit here, being looked at, but no one has ever come inside before. Now, you will stay for some tea, yes?"

"Please," said Katie.

"I have some cream cakes too. Now, *un* lump or *deux*?" asked Madame Moitessier, pointing to the sugar bowl.

"*Trois!*" said Katie.

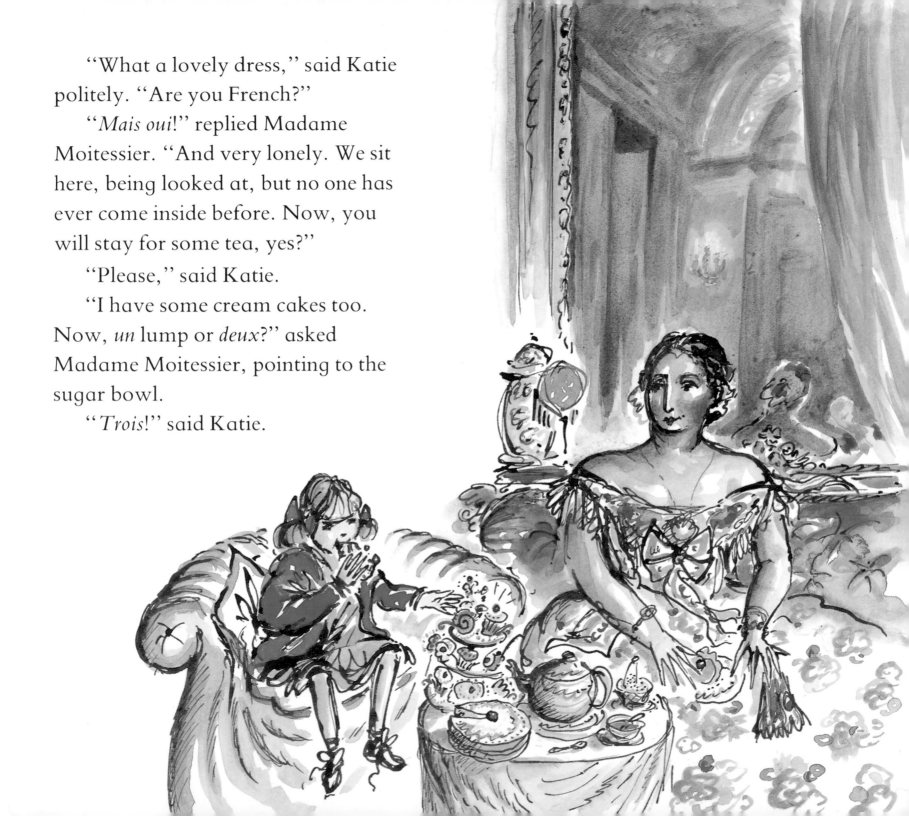

So they talked and talked. And they enjoyed themselves watching the surprised faces of the other visitors to the gallery.

"I have not laughed so much for years!" said Madame Moitessier. She was quite overcome. She had to use her fan to calm herself down.

But Katie laughed so much that she spilt her tea (it was her fourth cup) all over Madame Moitessier's dress.

"Oh, you clumsy child!" shrieked Madame Moitessier.

Katie, who had also managed to get mud all over the carpet, decided to leave. She helped herself to another cream cake, climbed out of the picture and back into the gallery.

Katie wandered into another room and went
straight up to the biggest picture.

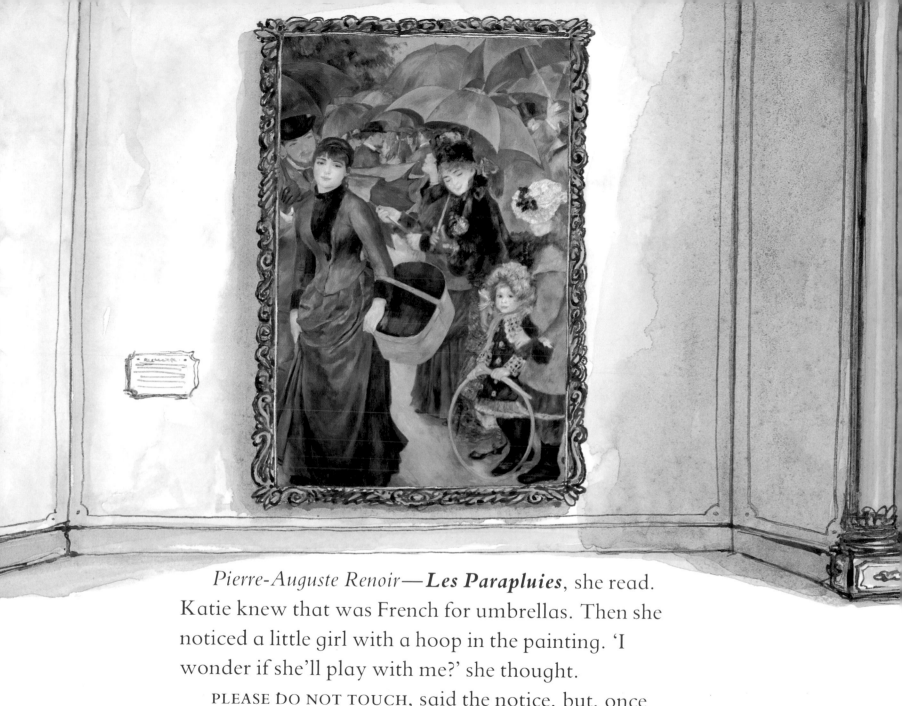

Pierre-Auguste Renoir—**Les Parapluies**, she read.
Katie knew that was French for umbrellas. Then she
noticed a little girl with a hoop in the painting. 'I
wonder if she'll play with me?' she thought.

PLEASE DO NOT TOUCH, said the notice, but, once
again, she did.

"Would you like a cream cake?" said Katie to the little girl.

"*Merci,*" she replied. "You can play with my hoop if you like."

Soon they were having quite a game, bowling the hoop to one another. All the other people watched from under their umbrellas.

But Katie hit the hoop too hard and it flew right out of the picture! It bounced on the floor and disappeared into another painting. The little girl started to cry.

"Whoops!" said Katie. "I'd better try to find it."
She jumped out of the Renoir painting and ran over
to the other picture.

Henri Rousseau, she read, **Tropical Storm With a Tiger**. PLEASE DO NOT TOUCH.

But Katie couldn't see the hoop, so she climbed over the frame and into the picture.

Katie found herself in a wild jungle. The wind blew and it was raining very hard. She was rather scared of the tiger, but he was even more scared of her. He ran off into the trees.

Katie still couldn't see the hoop, so she wandered off to explore.

Eventually she came to a lake full of crocodiles. They snapped their jaws at her, but Katie just laughed and climbed up a banana tree where they couldn't reach her. She helped herself to a banana.

Just then Katie saw the hoop hanging on a branch. She pulled it down and then found her way back to the picture frame, and jumped into the gallery.

Katie threw the hoop back into the Renoir picture.
"Here it is!" she said. The little girl was very
pleased. They waved goodbye to each other and
Katie ran off into the next room.

Exhibition of Modern Art, read Katie. *All the paintings are lent with kind permission.* DO NOT TOUCH.

Katie looked at a very different picture.

Kasimir Malevich, **Dynamic Suprematism**, she read. 'It would be fun to climb up that big triangle,' she thought.

Without checking to see if anyone was watching, she climbed inside the painting.

When Katie reached the big triangle, she climbed up to the top and slid down the other side.

"Wonderful!" she cried. This was the best picture yet.

But Katie couldn't stop and she fell further and further into the painting. It was like falling into a great big mouth.

"Help!" she cried. She was very scared. She didn't want to be eaten by a piece of modern art.

She heard a shout. "Hang on there!" It was the
guard. He threw a rope into the painting. Katie held
on to it with all her strength and the guard pulled her
back to the picture frame.

"That will teach you to obey notices," he said.

"Sorry," said Katie, who was covered in splodges
of paint. "I don't think I'll ever do that again."

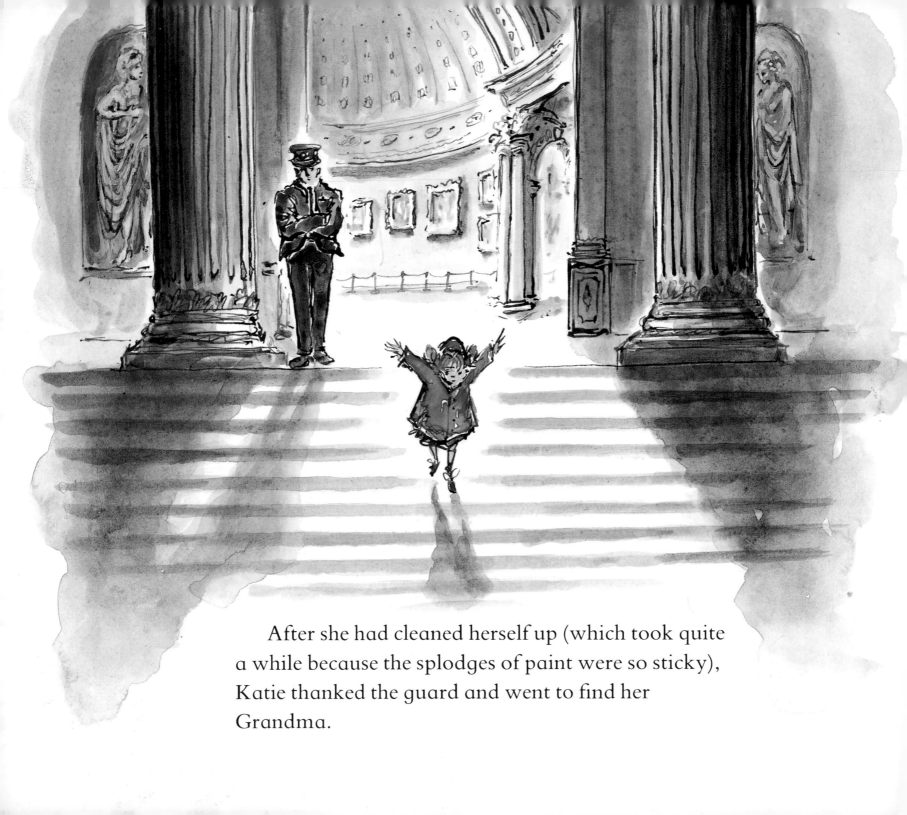

After she had cleaned herself up (which took quite
a while because the splodges of paint were so sticky),
Katie thanked the guard and went to find her
Grandma.

Grandma was snoozing on a comfortable chair.
"You're late," she said when Katie woke her. "I hope you had a nice time."

"Yes, thanks," said Katie. "I really like looking at pictures."

It had stopped raining now. So, after Katie had bought postcards of her favourite pictures, they went to find a cup of tea and a cream cake.

More about Katie's pictures

Katie's pictures are:

The Hay Wain
by *John Constable* (1776–1837)
in the National Gallery, London

Madame Moitessier Seated
by *Jean-Auguste-Dominique Ingres*
(1780–1867)
in the National Gallery, London

Les Parapluies
by *Pierre-Auguste Renoir* (1841–1919)
in the National Gallery, London

Tropical Storm With a Tiger
by *Henri Rousseau* (1844–1910)
in the National Gallery, London

Dynamic Suprematism
by *Kasimir Malevich* (1878–1935)
in the Tate Gallery, London

As Katie discovered, art galleries are full of wonderful paintings to enjoy. You will have to visit London to see the real paintings in this book, but there is sure to be a museum or gallery near you where there are other interesting pictures to see. Many of them will have a special children's guide.

Although in the story Katie did touch the paintings, you must not. This is because the paintings are all very precious and could easily be damaged.

Don't try to look at too many paintings on one visit—just choose a few, as Katie did, and look at all the detail, shapes and colours.

All artists have a different way of seeing the world around them. If you paint a picture, it won't look anything like the one a friend might paint. James Mayhew painted the pictures of Katie and her adventures and you will see that these pictures look different from the five paintings Katie climbed into.

So, when you visit an art gallery, look really hard at the paintings and see how much you can find out about the way each artist paints!